Bumble Bear

POINTING THE WAY

WRITTEN BY JAMES HOFFMAN   ILLUSTRATED BY JOHN SANDFORD

Dedicated to one of my cubs,
Geoffrey.
J.D.H.

For Sarah Spahn Smith,
The Countess of McLean County.
J.S.

Bumble Bear loved honey. The cottage where he lived with his family had shelf upon shelf of honey jars. Oh, there were jars filled with raspberry and strawberry jam, but the honey jars were empty. Bumble Bear usually bumbled his plans to fill those jars with honey. His wife, Gwendolyn, and his cubs, Wear and Tear, kindly said nothing. Bumble Bear's stomach always rumbled for honey.

Bumble Bear spent hours trying to learn the secrets of getting honey.
He buzzed through his drawings and books about bees and hives.
Over and over he mumbled, "Where bees *are*, honey *is*."
Then one day, he looked at the two basic rules on his wall:
"*Where hives are, bees are*," and "*Where bees and hives are, honey is*."
"Hives, therefore, are full of honey,"
thought Bumble Bear.

A honey of an idea swarmed into his head. "Maybe I can get the bees to move!" he shouted, and started planning and drawing and talking to himself. "They'll move into *my* hive, and then I'll have *their* hive. A bee-utiful hive full of honey!"

With a towering stack of plans, Bumble Bear marched into his workshop. Wear and Tear and Gwendolyn Bear heard sawing and hammering and, once, a great roar—Bumble Bear had fumbled, hitting his paw with the hammer.

At last, the door to the workshop burst open. Bumble Bear marched
out with an armful of signs and a crazy, hive-like contraption.
Down to the meadow he went with the new hive and signs.

Some of the signs were just pictures, in case the bees couldn't read. "But bees *are* smart," thought Bumble Bear. That's why he had made some signs with words, too. And all of them pointed the way to the wonderful new hive.

At the end of his trail of signs, Bumble Bear placed the new hive
he had made and the last sign, which read, "*Comb, sweet comb.*"
He scratched his head as he looked at it. "It just doesn't
look *quite* as good as a *natural* hive," he thought.
"Ah! Maybe that is because a real hive is full of honey!"

Bumble Bear waited
by the new hive all day
with hopes that the bees
would soon arrive.

But the bees did not follow the signs. They did not move into their new home. Off in the distance, though, at the old hive, Bumble Bear thought he heard hammering and sawing.

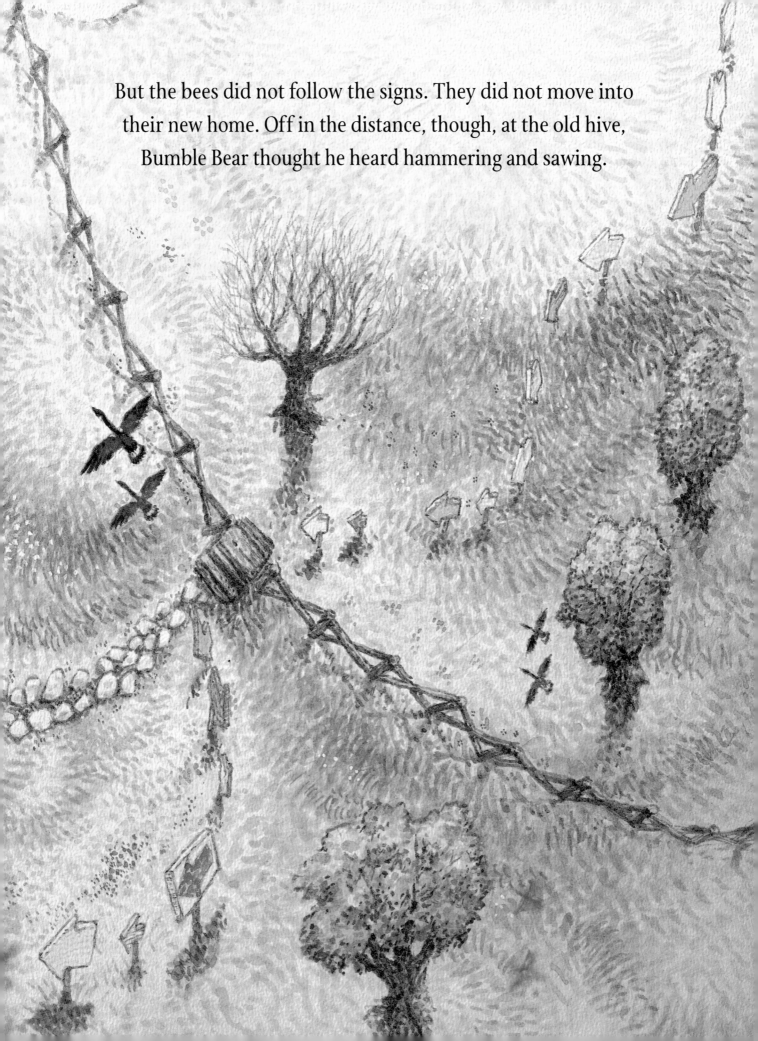

The next morning, Bumble Bear looked into the empty new hive. "Time for another plan," he said, and taking the wheelbarrow, he headed down to the meadow. "Those bees are moving whether they like it or not," he grumbled.

Bumble Bear had planned to wheel the bees straight to their new home. When he got to the hive, he wrapped his arms around it and lifted it up. Suddenly, Bumble Bear found himself in a cloud of angry bees!

Buzzing furiously, the bees formed an arrow, and Bumble Bear took the hint. He started to run in the direction the bees pointed—straight towards the forest.

As he hurried and stumbled and ran and tumbled, he noticed the bees had made signs of their own! He followed those signs straight up a tree, tearing his clothes as he climbed higher and higher. "Bumbled again," he thought, peering out from the leaves, watching the bees.

Later, when the coast was clear, Bumble Bear trudged home in his underwear, grumbling. Wear and Tear and Gwendolyn Bear watched from the cottage windows, not saying a word.

That night, Bumble Bear started thinking and studying and planning again. "*Next* time..." he mumbled. "Just wait until *next* time."

Gwendolyn carried a tray of goodies to Bumble Bear as he sat
in the cozy living room of Honey Hill Cottage.
"What a humbled honey he is,"
she thought.

She smiled and said,
"I have a sweet surprise. Wear and Tear
were given a big comb of honey in return for the gift
of your homemade hive. The bees will use it for extra storage!"